SACR
S
D0382414

FRIENDS

AIKO IKEGAMI

ALBERT WHITMAN & COMPANY
CHICAGO, ILLINOIS

I would like to thank Mark Mitchell, Julie Lake, Anna Olswanger, Jordan Kost, Wendy McClure, and Albert Whitman & Company for helping me to make this book complete.—Al

To all of my friends

Library of Congress Cataloging-in-Publication data
is on file with the publisher.

Text and pictures copyright © 2016 by Aiko Ikegami
Published in 2016 by Albert Whitman & Company
ISBN 978-0-8075-2550-0
All rights reserved. No part of this book may be reproduced or transmitted in any form or by any means, electronic or mechanical, including photocopying, recording, or by any information storage and retrieval system, without permission in writing from the publisher.

Printed in China
10 9 8 7 6 5 4 3 2 1 LP 24 23 22 21 20 19 18 17 16 15

Design by Jordan Kost

For more information about Albert Whitman & Company,
visit our web site at www.albertwhitman.com.

One day...

Aa Dd Ee Ff Ii Jj
A NEW STUDENT CAME.

She was different.

And alone.

She wanted someone who could be a friend.

Someone to eat with.

One day...

Someone came to visit.

And stayed to eat.

AND PLAY.

Another friend came.

More friends came.

THEY ALL STAYED TO PLAY.

Then a new student came.

Aa Dd Ee Ff Ii Jj
HE WAS DIFFERENT.

But he stayed too.

And they all played.